Walk Wit' Me

The Widows Mind

Latanya Jackson

Walk Wit' Me
Copyright © 2011 by Latanya Jackson

ISBN 978-0-615-44264-8

Printed in USA by 48HrBooks (www.48HrBooks.com)

This book is a work of fiction. It is not meant to depict, portray or represent any particular real persons. All the characters, incidents and dialogues are products of the author's imagination and are not to be construed as real. Any references or similarities to actual events, entities, real people, living or dead, or to real locales are intended to give the novel a sense of reality. Any similarity in other names, characters, entities, places and incidents are entirely coincidental.

My heart knows what wants to be written but as I sit here looking at this blank screen I'm blank, feelings of anger, hurt, abandonment and sadness are all present yet I still don't know where to begin. So while I'm letting the emotions simmer I'll start with why this book finally made its way out.

I first and foremost want to apologize to my babies for keeping the truth hidden for so long. I really thought it was best at the time. Mom, Dad I never had the chance to really thank you and even though I know you guys know it THANK YOU!!!!!! For making me the person I am. James D Jackson Jr (Pop), you will always be a part of my life; I really wouldn't have it any other way. Virginia Jackson (Ma) what can I say but you told me so. Brian, my brother and friend all I can say is I Love You; no matter what the weather was like you kept the umbrella from flying away. Kerry in my heart you were still a friend of mine I'm sorry we couldn't get it right.

My sisters for Tyeisha Roker a.k.a Tye (u already know, we go back to the days when Freaky Ty was laid out on the couch, and taking cabs to Gabby's just cause the munchies were calling) Kelly Smith (my cousin and respirator thank you for being the ear and logic) Cynthia Eastman (we had some crazy days and long nights but oh what fun we had) Takeeyah Lee Jeffries (need I say why. OKAY getting straight to the point you were the only real nigga in the equation) Eightball, you were more like a fresh breath of air than a friend. You saw a part of me that no one else recognized; and caused me to think more than I cared to at the time. You showed genuine concern and for that you are my friend for life. Lemound Nickay Scott you probably weren't ready or you just didn't believe me but truth be told you were really "THE ONE" …Eric, you was

4

the push I needed and I may or may never get to say this but I Love You Friend…... It is what it is!

I want to thank the many people whom God put in my life at the times he did and thank him for opening my eyes to the ones that were a health hazard. This has been a road with many turns and unexpected drops but with the grace of God and the many angels he kept present it wasn't a journey taken alone.

Above everything I thank God for the strength, wisdom and determination he gave me. There were many days that his love alone carried me.

I would like to give special shout outs to

Mitchel "Blaze" Myree, Sami "Peanut" Myree, , Joseph
Myree, Tito Myree, Christrian Myree, Ebony "Big Eb"
Myree, David Myree, Ebony "Muya" Myree, Albert
Myree, Pernell Myree, Waheedah Stevenson, Brian Daley,
Christine Capers, Storm Jefferson, Widad Abdul-Saleem,
Aunt Gracie, Aunt Janice, Aunt Elaine, Muslima Ansari,
Ashley McCrory, Mark Sams, Yetta Coleman, Shawna
Jones, Kendra Morris, Karrin Morris, Wanda Smith
Subero, Cieara Stokes, Duane Price……….

Nobody was left out intentionally; so don't take it
personally!

Dedications!
This book is dedicated to three kings and a princess……
Hahsan Infinite Jackson, Qudar Amir Jackson,
James Dempsey Jackson IV and Tyana Mariam Jackson
And
In Loving Memory of
James Dempsey Jackson III
2/17/1973 ~ 8/1/2006

Stephanie Denise Myree
1/31/1984 ~ 4/28/2008

Stephan Isiah Myree
8//2006 ~ 4/28/2008

Chapter 1

"The Widows Mind"

Knock, knock Ma'am can we have a word with you

Are you Mrs. Sean Wilson,

Ma'am I'm sorry but he's been in an accident

Huh! What are you talking about, where is he...take me to

him, take me now!

Ma'am you're not listening he's gone! GONE? ....

My head is spinning I can't hear

My heart is heavy, I'm weak, my mouth is moving but there

are no words; I can't speak.

I'm walking, dialing wrong numbers, crying; now I

shout….. I want to see my husband

my heart is so heavy, when will this pain end

I want to wake up and it be a nightmare

this pain I can't bear.................Silence!

Loneliness turns to bitterness, bitterness to anger

Anger to aggression... Man I need a session

I feel stuck

No way out; can't go around it; got to go through it

I'm lost

Alone in a world where there's a million people around

Is this real or is this fake

Step in the mind of a widow and it's the longest walk you'll

take

"Hello! Hello Eight?"

"Who did you say you were looking for?"

"I'm sorry I think I dialed the wrong number. I was looking for an old friend."

"It's okay sweetie you know they say things happen for a Reason. You sound a little troubled, have you been crying."

"I really appreciate your kindness but I don't want to impose on you."

"You're not imposing at all there's always a reason for everything and God sure told me to take this call. But you never answered my question?"

"I'm sorry Ma'am what was the question again."

"Have you been crying? And no need to call me ma'am everyone calls me 'Momma T'. So are those tears I hear in your voice?

"Yes, I can't seem to stop them from falling. I've been

holding them back for so long that now I just can't stop them. Every little thing makes me cry. It's like what did I do so badly in my past life to warrant such a pain stricken life.

"Don't say that; the devil wants you to give up."

"Well baby let's start with your name and what or who you're crying about."

"Momma T my name is Storm and it's over my husband, for my kids and because of the never ending adversaries."

"You sound so young, excuse me for asking but how old are you?"

"I'm thirty two Ma'am."

"How long has it been?"

"It's been thirty five months and thirty days since my husband passed away and I'm still feeling the pain as if that day keeps repeating itself. It's like any little thing that happens triggers a wave of pain. I just want to get past the hurt and over the pain and back on my feet again. I want to live and feel alive, but there's this dark cloud that keeps following me."

"Storm baby I'm not going to sit here and say that I know what you're going through because no one knows your struggles but you; what I can give you is an ear to get some of that grief off your chest. How old are your kids?"

"They are nine, seven and four; they're my reason for not giving up completely but I have to be honest I'm so close to throwing my hand in. I just can't win for trying. I take two steps forward and get knocked ten steps back."

"Ain't that the truth, honey, I sure do know what you mean."

"Momma T please pray for me."

"Sure baby! 'Lord Jesus Christ, King of kings, you have power over life and death. You know even things that are uncertain and obscure, and our very thoughts and feelings are not hidden from you. Cleanse her from her pain and secret faults, guide her oh father for she is troubled and her heart is weary. Lord give her guidance and strength to carry out your task for she is diligently seeking to find her way through you. Lord father God watch over her and her children for the devil is a liar and he cannot have this child of yours. In Jesus name we pray Amen."

"Amen.

Momma T thank you, thank you for being the receiver of this call. I appreciate you giving your time so freely."

"Sure baby it was my pleasure; anytime you need to talk don't hesitate to call me. Matter of fact I'll be calling you."

"Okay, Momma T I didn't realize how late it was." "It is pretty late."

"I'm going to let you get some rest."

"Alright Storm, but we still have so much to talk about."

"Why you say that?"

"Well for one I don't know how you and your husband met or how he passed. The kids' names. All I know is that you're too young to be going at this alone. Pain if held too tight can be a damaging thing for anyone. Did you seek counseling? Are you even from Georgia? Have any family or friends here? Even though they can be more detrimental than helpful. Have you tried to move on?"

"Wow it's been a long time since anyone has really asked me about me and really cared to know. Honestly, Momma T this is a pretty long story and it's got more twists and turns than the average roller coaster. I'm just now getting to the point where I can talk about some of the details and not cry. Shit I programmed myself on how to hold it in."

"Well baby as old as I am, I don't have anything but time on my hands and the Lord put us on the same line tonight for a reason. For you it could be a step towards healing and for me; well he knows exactly why he woke me up. So Storm, are you going to make an old lady wait longer than she has to. We're already up so come on get to singing. And don't be trying to change up how you would normally talk; act like I'm the gentleman you were looking for."

"Who, Eight?"

"Eight, yes I believe that's the name you said. I guess I'll find out who he is soon enough."

I met Eight at a spot called Dudley's out in Lithonia. While out in the parking lot over walks the muscular light skinned cutie I admired from afar in the club. So while my peoples and his squabbled childishly we walked off to exchange numbers. Momma T he was so hot, we talked on the phone that night for hours. He understood the pain I carried underneath and was open to the terms I thought I wanted at the time.

His caring was something I needed internally. For a man to genuinely show concern about what I was going through. Taking the time to talk to me and hear me. I started loving him for him. For the person he was to me gave me a glimpse of hope that my heart wasn't completely gone.

Eight was a good man and wonderful friend. Yet he was

someone I used selfishly for my wants and he still remained

my friend after it all.

"But Momma T he doesn't come in the picture any time

soon."

"Well I'm sure he's important nevertheless."

"Yes ma'am he was."

"Hold on baby let Momma T get herself situated here.

Okay Storm I'm ready, and remember just let it go!"

Chapter 2

"Some could say that the signs were there; others can say that they never seen it coming. I can say that you never know what someone is going through no matter how close you are to them. Sometimes things just happen that you have no control over; no matter what you feel could have been done differently to change the outcome, it is what it is. I let many precious minutes, hours and years fly by because I couldn't bring myself to let go of the anger. How selfish of him to determine when I didn't need my husband and our kids need their father. The anger consumed me to the point of no return.

I sank; I sank so quickly that I couldn't even feel myself going under. Through depression and guilt I closed my eyes to the world and escaped into a pit of darkness. It was in the pit that I was introduced to counterfeit joy. The kind of joy that comes with the illusion that all things happening are good. Now pay attention to how I break shit down because I really do have a way with words. I like to play with them. Walk through the pit with me for a hot minute. I've been holding this shit in for so long that I'm a beast changing under the moon."

"Girl you sure do sound like it, like you were just waiting to be asked the right questions."

"Well Momma T the first stop was on Phony Street. That's where I received those fake bills. That metaphor is talking about females, dudes. Shit whoever is phony and try to act like they so straight up."

"Child you sure got some way with words."

"Told you I like to play with them; makes understanding things interesting. Anyways, the ill part of that was I had those bills put away on some rainy day shit, and the minute I needed to bust them they were revealed as no good. Momma T meaning…"

"…girl hush I ain't slow."

"See I moved out to the A in fall of "05" that's when I came across them bills; now I didn't think anything then because I came across them with mutual interests. But never would I have guessed that those bills were as phony as the mother fuckers who claimed them. Check how I found this shit out. When my husband and I moved from NY there was nothing in the A for me but my husband Sean our sons at that time Justice was 12, Malik 6, King 5 and our princess Nyima was 1. Although there was nothing for me Sean had family and a few friends out here. His cousin Jason had his wifey and kids here and his friend Dante' from back home was here with his girl Lana.

The first day we touched down we went by his homeboy Dante' spot. You know to check the layout of the apartment, peep the neighborhood. Just to get a feel of where we wanted to rest at. Once we left there, we headed over to his cousin Jasons' house. They lived in Decatur. That's when I was introduced to Kia for the 2nd time; we first met back in NY at a father's day cookout around the way. Kia is Jasons' wife.

Immediately Kia and I hit it off, started hanging real tight. On some if I eat you eat type shit. Holidays was spent at each other's' spot, birthday parties, cookouts, shopping on no budgets, nails on a weekly. I mean really getting it in. Going hard like we knew each other for years. It didn't matter there was never a time that Kia couldn't come to me for help and not get it. I'm just built that way; anyone who ever got to really know me know that if you my nigga you my nigga and it should be vice versa.

Unfortunately shit doesn't always go that smooth. So if you never heard this shit before, pay attention. Whenever you are doing good there is always that one Hater plotting your disaster."

"Well baby that's one thing you surely don't have to tell this old bitty. I've had my share of users pretending to be friends. But go on."

"After a while Sean decided that it was best to be closer to everyone; since he would soon be dipping in and out of town. He wanted to feel secure in knowing that if there was ever a problem, I wasn't too far away from family. So when we moved to Decatur we just coincidently moved in the same hood as Candice and Mark. Those are Jason's peoples from his old neighborhood back up north. It was on and poppin' then. We didn't have to drive far to chill with niggas. The kids had more friends. And now here comes hatin' ass Kia. For a while we lived on the other side of I285 so Kia for the most part really had this friend to herself. I just wasn't aware that she wanted to keep it that way and by any means necessary.

Check this bitch out, actin' like we was in a

relationship or something. The minute I got cool with some of her home girls she started throwing salt on their name. *"Storm don't be getting caught up with them they don't like you"*, my ass would be like "aight that's what's up". A bitch like me is straight on the friend shit. Here her silly ass goes saying they were like that with me when I first came on the scene. So here I am thinking; then you dumb as fuck. And if you know so much about what they be saying about me; then bitch you be right there with them too.

She would always try to sugar coat it, like them acting that way with her initially was supposed to be some type of reassurance that she was on my side."
"And ain't that the Gods honest truth; baby I'm old and don't get why some women feel they have to be conniving to survive."
"She use to go so hard, I remember her saying, "Storm just

forget them bitches they just mad they ain't doing it like you. We cool and that's all that matters; those bitches ain't going to ever say the shit to your face. And they know to cease that bullshit when I walk in the room", then my reply was "I'm a leave it alone for now; after all at the end of the day I really don't give a fuck. But on a serious note Kia I'm a see her about me being the hot topic".

That way when I do decide the time is right, you already knew I said it was going to happen. Storm you know I told you, I don't say shit I can't repeat. Fuck them bitches."

"So are you and Kia still friends now?"

"Momma T you'll find out soon enough."

"Did you confront them, girl you can't keep an old lady in suspense?"

"No Momma T I did just the opposite, shit no reason in me coming out my character on some he say she say shit.

Don't get it twisted though I kept that on the back burner;

but I definitely was that bitch that you were going to love to

hate and hate that you loved. Over the months it was just

like that. It was first the stares and whispers at the

functions. Then it was the everybody like Storm wagon.

Even though things were cool after a while, I still had that

one un-resolved issue.

I've only been in the A about five months and

already have an envious snake breeding hater in my midst.

Besides that I couldn't wait for my home girl to move

down here. They thought they couldn't stand me. Shit me

and Star was one in the same, somewhat; I guess. Then

again we have had our share of silent fallen outs. You know

the she so mad she gets stuck on Mad Lane. You get

sentenced to indefinite silence. Sort of like Fed time."

"Huh? Now that one you're going to have to tell me about

that one."

"Okay you know how the state will get you on every little thing you do and punish you do then. Well the Feds will sit back and watch your ass and let everything pile up; then put your ass under the jail and sentence you to like 300 yrs."

"Alright I get you and that's how Star is I take it." "Yes Ma'am she is."

"Well did your friend ever make it out here?"

"Yeah she made it out here. But we're no longer the friends we were at least not on her end. And I'm not one of them begging type bitches so I just left it alone. It's fucked up it had to be that way but; anyways... Moving past that, Momma T its four o'clock in the morning you're not tired yet."

"No baby I'm actually enjoying our conversation. Don't you feel a little bit better?"

"Yes ma'am it does feel good to vent a little."

"So now tell me again why you are still holding back."

"Huh?"

"You heard me, when are you going to let the pain go. What we talked about wasn't what brought you pain, that bitch excuse my French was just a devil in disguise."

"Well I hope you have some Kleenex by your bed, we both about to do some heavy crying. Hold on a sec Let me grab my journal."

"Your journal?"

"Yeah Momma T it'll take you there a little better hearing it in narrator mode. Trust me!"

"Okay baby, I'm ready when you are."

As I take in a deep breath and exhale slow...... "Here we go! Be prepared to cry!"

Chapter 3

August 1, 2006 that date will forever be a constant reminder of how one day can change every aspect of life as you know it. It's been two years and 11 months and 19 days and I remember every detail of every minute.

Just like any morning for the past three weeks, Sean woke me up before leaving out to work. "Storm, baby" he would say. "You know I love you right? God forbid anything was to ever happen to me. I want you to know that I Love You! I want you to promise me that you will always believe that." "Baby I will never doubt your love for me. We said it from day one. Sean it's me and you; ain't nothing stopping that."

"Alright baby I'm a head to work, I'm giving notice today. I really need to start focusing on our business."

"Sean you know I'm down no matter what, haven't I always?" "That's why you my partner Mrs. Sean Wilson. Come walk me to the door." "Okay baby see you later", we exchange kisses and break away. As I walked back to the bedroom I checked on the little ones, they still sleep. Cool I can get my ass back in the bed for a about another hour.

"Yo son that shit is hot; we need to jump on that now. Get things going. For real." I can hear Sean and one of his partners in the living room. Damn he back already? What time is it? I was sleep that long? "Hold on son let me go holla at wifey a sec." "Aight I'm here my dude. I'm a get on the internet and look some of this shit up." "Cool."

"Boo! Wake up I gotta run some of this stuff pass you. You know you're the right side of my brain, shit don't work right without your input." "Boy whatever", I was all cheesing and shit. "What you got to tell me, you love me." "You already know that. Remember I told you I was giving

31

notice today." "Yeah. Well He was actually very understanding about the whole situation so today will be my last day with his company. I'm going full steam ahead with our shit. This is going to happen, I see it." "Well you already know I'm with you." "I know that's why I need you to do another presentation and a grant proposal. You know it's going to cost you a trip to Lenox." "I bet it is."

"So what ya'll got going on in there?" Oh, me and Kev about to draft up this 12 city tour and gather a street team. Cool I'll be out there in a sec, let me throw something on and get my mouth right. Please do I didn't want to say anything, but! yeah you need to handle that.

"Storm it sounds like you and your husband really loved each other." "I thought so too." "You don't now?" "Momma T there was a time when I thought I knew, but unfortunately that's not how I was left feeling. One moment took away a vision that was once so clear."

"Oh, baby what happened? You sound like you want to cry now. Stop holding it in. If you need to cry, cry. You have to let yourself let go. Before your pain becomes your death. You think he would want you to be hurting like this. Living just because. You are young and still can have happiness if you let it in. but you have to first let go of that brick you holding onto."

"Momma T it's honestly easier said than done. Matter of fact that's all anybody ever says. But truth is; it's not that easy. When you carry a pain so deep, it's hard to swallow. Let alone move past it as quick as people say it should happen. You never understand why people shut themselves off from the world until you go through what they do. Well I've been there and you'll be there too. Just keep listening."

No matter how much I try to pretend like

Everything's okay, everyday my heart is heavy...It's like

every day at some point in the day I re-live the same

moment.....Here is that moment!

As I sat at the desk typing one of the many essays due Sunday night the kids were in their room playing; the commotion outside caused the little nosey ones to go running out to see what happened. DeKalb County came in the complex 3 cars deep running like chickens with they heads cut off. As the kids ran out I yelled for them to get back inside.

"Get yo' asses back in here you don't know who the hell they looking for and why." While I stood on the patio the officers ran into our building; in less than two seconds they were standing in my door way asking if they could have a word with me in private, so I told the kids to go back outside.

One of the officers took out his notepad and asked me did I know Mr. Sean Wilson; immediately I went into why you want to know mode. "Yes, why? What's the problem?" *"How do you know him Ma'am?"* was their response. "I'm his wife now what's the problem and where is he?" *"Ma'am when you open his wallet what is the first thing you see?"* "Our family photo… now tell me what's going on." *"Ma'am he's been in an accident."*

I went numb, sat down on the couch and then reached for the phone. See I was under the impression that he was helping his best friend move; so I thought is everybody else alright. The officer then said *'Ma'am you're not listening you have to let me finish.'* 'Where is he? Take me to him; I want to see my husband now.' *'Ma'am,'* the officer said *'I'm sorry but he's gone…'* 'GONE!' That shit just wasn't registering. 'What the hell you mean gone?!' *'Ma'am he was found in a company van in the parking lot of the old bowling alley. Do you know why he would be there?'*

'What? I don't even know where the old bowling alley was.' *'Ma'am, it appears that he committed suicide.'* Did he just say what I thought he said?

My heart dropped................

I couldn't hear, talk, or think; I was frozen still. My heart started hurting, I couldn't breathe, I felt like I was taking my last breathe. I put my hand on my heart while I tried to control my heavy breathing. I was gasping for air. My whole world just came crumbling and all I felt was pain. *"Ma'am are you alright? Would you like to go to the hospital? Ma'am?"* The officers just calling out to me

He didn't kill himself; he said he would never take himself away from me and our kids. He made me promise him. *"Ma'am I'm sorry what does that mean? He made you promise?"* We talked about this three weeks ago. He told me he felt like he was going to die soon. He didn't know when and he didn't know why. That no matter what anybody tells me or how it looks. He would never take himself away from me and the kids. That somebody would have to force him out of this world. Nope! I don't believe that. Get out; get the fuck outta my house! *"Ma'am is there anyone you can call?"* the one person I want to call is dead. I remember walking to my bedroom like a zombie and just staring at the spot on the bed that would now be empty; hearing the officers follow me asking me is there someone I can call. All I could think was, *'these bastards*; how dare they say that'. Why are you following me?

I thought I told you to leave. I want you out of my house. *"Ma'am I know this is hard but we have to ask you some questions. Did you and your husband have any problems?"* What the fuck you mean did we have

problems; matter of fact don't ask me shit. Just get out!

All I could think about was what about my kids, how

will I be able to tell them that their father is gone. Then it

really hit and I could not stop the crying. I'm trying to call

my father-in-law and can't seem to find his number; what is

his number. Here, I handed the officer the phone look for

pop duke and hit talk. *"Huh ma'am?"* Dial my father-in-

law. I can't stop crying long enough to see. I'm on the

phone with my father-in-law and I can't even speak those

words into existence all I could do was cry while trembling

uncontrollably trying to say pop. 'Storm, what's wrong

baby.'

'Here you tell him' I handed the phone to the officer

as I walked away. What am I going to tell our kids, how

can I look at them and not cry. *Come on Storm get yourself*

together, is all I kept trying to tell myself but my insides were burning. My heart felt like it was in my stomach. I was just empty. '*Ma'am your father-in-law wants you,*' 'baby I'll be there in the morning, I'm coming.' Through tears he's apologizing for my pain and all I could do was cry.

'*Ma'am is there anyone that can be with you now? Is there anyone else you can call? You don't need to be alone right now.*' As I walked out the apartment I swallowed hard and wiped my face; but I couldn't hide the fact that I was crying. 'Ma what's wrong?' 'Auntie Storm why were you crying?' 'Take the kids to Auntie Candice house and tell her to come quick it's an emergency.'

Candice and Mark came running down to our building. '*Storm what's wrong? What's going on? Where's Sean?*' And that's when it all came out, at that very moment as I spoke I went down. '*He's gone, they said he's gone, my husband is gone'* was all I could say over and

over. *'What?'* *'Candice they said he's dead.'* *'Oh my God,*

Storm I'm so sorry." She grabbed hold of me and

comforted me through the cries. *'They won't take me to*

him; I just want to see my husband. Please just take me to

him.' *'Ma'am you won't be able to see him right now.'*

'Why? I want my husband; I just want my husband.'

I called my parents and my father answered, he heard

me crying and said *'girl what's the matter with you?'*

'Daddy he's gone.' *'Who's gone? What you talking about?'*

'He's dead daddy. Sean's dead.' *'Oh baby no, ya'll just left*

here; Oh Storm, baby. I'm sorry, what happened? We

coming baby. I'm calling your mother now.'

With eight kids total in my home I'm in pain and

have to be strong." "Eight? I thought you said you only had

four." "Yes; well that particular year we had two of our

nieces come stay with us for the summer and coupled with that a cousin and Justices' friend was spending the night. So not only did I have to worry about how mine were going to take the news."

"Well you sure did have your hands full. I don't know how I would've been. That's for sure." Momma T added.

"Well Candice and Mark made the calls to let our people in ATL know what happened," I continued. "Matter of fact Candice did most of the calling. I guess she just went through the phone. I really don't remember calling anyone after my parents. As I started to walk off Candice grabbed for my arm; '*Storm where are you going? I have to see my husband, I just need to go. Storm you don't have any shoes on. I don't care I just want to go. Tell me where the bowling alley was so I can go. Storm he's not there anymore they already took him to the morgue. Candice I*

42

just want my husband. Why him? Why?'

While Candice stayed consoling me, Mark was talking with the officers. They told Mark that he killed himself, that it appeared that he put the gun to his mouth and blew his brains out. What the fuck. What kind of shit is that to say? How the hell do you sit there and tell somebody some bullshit like that. *'I want them to get the fuck away from here. Tell them to go; before I go off. They won't let me see him and they being rude on top of that.'*

One of the officers then came over to me; I'm thinking, *what the hell does he want now? He already said what he needed to. 'Mrs. Wilson, again I'm sorry for your loss and if there is anything I can do please don't hesitate to call me. Here's my card and I'm also going to give you my cell phone number. Please Mrs. Wilson don't hesitate to call. The medical examiner will be contacting you later this*

43

evening and they'll give you the details of their findings.'
Through teary eyes, all I could do was stare and nod. I still couldn't believe that I was living this nightmare.

'Storm here the medical examiner is on the phone.'
'Hello,' I stated. 'Hi Mrs. Wilson this is Medical Examiner John Sparks I would like to talk to you about your late husband Mr. Sean Wilson. We huve him here at the office and upon our findings it appears that your husband did in fact commit suicide,' He said politely. 'Well then I don't think you have anything to say to me. I know he didn't do that.' Was my response.

'He said he would never take his life away from us. 'I continued. 'So when you do know what happened call me back save this bullshit for someone else.' 'Ma'am I understand you're upset.' 'No, you don't. Where is your office located so I can come see him?' 'Ma'am you won't *be able to see him until you make arrangements for his*

body to be moved to the funeral home.' 'So you're telling

me that I have to plan his funeral before I know for sure

that it's him you have...' 'It's against GA state rules to

allow you in here. You have to have all the necessary

shots.' 'What the hell do I need shots for? He's dead. What

the fuck can I possibly give him? Or anybody there for that

matter. I don't even want to talk to you anymore. Here,' I

passed the phone to Mark. 'You can talk to his dumb ass he

pissing me off.'

While were standing around outside all I hear is

'*Nooooooooooo!!*'; I can hear my oldest screaming. As I'm

running back into the house all I could think was *who the*

fuck told him?

Justice, Destiny and Angel were in the house

apparently when it all happened one of Justice Friends' was

still in the house so he heard mostly everything the officers said. Justice kept on asking Kevin what happened, '*what happened to my mother?*' He didn't want to tell them but, they wouldn't let up. They wanted to know why I was crying. '*What did they say to make my mother cry like that?*' Kevin was like '*man go ask your mother I don't want to be the one to say it.*' '*If you don't tell me I'm going to bust you in yo' mouth,*' gnarled Justice. Kevin said '*man Justice yo' daddy gone! man, yo daddy gone.*'

Angel was hollering and destiny was laid out on the floor screaming '*my uncle; I want my uncle.*' Justice in such a rage punched a hole in the wall and jumped out the window. I ran back out the house to get him and all I could do was hold him through his screams.

I'm crying because I feel his pain and I'm mad. *How dare he do this to us? Like you asshole, did you foresee this outcome? Did you factor this shit into your equation?*

'Justice, baby we have to be strong for your brothers and sister.'- I told him through his screams as I held on. *Oh my God* was all I could think. He wasn't supposed to find out like this.

'Justice come on, I know this is a lot. But please for me. Calm down. I know you're hurting but I need your help. Your brothers and sister still don't know yet and I need more time.' Damn it! How am I going to be able to tell them that their father isn't coming home ever again? Just to think it, is heart breaking. But now I have to look at them in their innocent eyes and break their hearts. Poor little souls are going to be crushed. Shit, Justice is just a baby his damn self and here I am needing him to toughen up. Sean damn you for this, Damn you.

'Storm come on think, get yourself together.' That's all I kept saying. Fuck it let me call this bitch and tell her that her son needs her. She better not piss me off, today is not

the day.

'Hello, hey Craig this is Storm I've been trying to reach
Tane' but she keep sending me to the damn voice mail, it's
an emergency something happened to Sean. So can you tell
her that she needs to call me right away.'"

'"So Tane' is your husbands baby momma" asked
Momma T. "Yes that's Justice mother. Well the stupid
bitch finally called back yelling into the damn phone.
'What happened to my son, if anything happened to my son
it's going to be a fucking problem.' So I was like *'first off*
who the fuck are you talking to. You ain't doing shit to
nobody so bitch shut the fuck up and listen. Ain't shit
happen to your son. My husband is dead.

That's why I was calling your dumb ass. To tell you
your son needs you right now. But you would have known

that if your trifling ass would have picked up the phone.
You don't know what the fuck we were calling for. It could
have been about your son. But if you cared that much you
would have answered the first damn time.' I scoffed. 'Oh
storm I'm sorry I didn't know. I apologize.' Man I didn't
want to hear shit she was saying at that time. I chucked that
phone clear in the woods.

Then on top of dealing with that bitch I'm getting
stupid ass calls from another dumb broad up north saying
she heard I had something to do with it. What? Did this
bitch really try me like that? Clearly they didn't know
today was not the day. I would have surely caught a case."

"Are you serious? Storm they didn't do that. With all
that you were going through. They were bringing you
bullshit like that." – Momma T said. "Man Momma T I had
to tell those dudes, if they come down here I'm fucking

49

them up. They're not invited to the funeral; I don't want to see them. Keep them messy bitches away from me. For real; for real."

"So did they come? Shit I don't know why I asked you that. You probably wouldn't be telling me this story right now." Momma T laughed a little. "Pretty much. My ass would have been checked in at Memorial Inn for sure. DeKalb would have put me under the jail."

"Well, what gave them the impression that you were the cause when he checked himself out?" asked Momma T. "Well at the time I thought it was because his baby momma called Justice back on the sneak tip asking him a shit load of questions and learned that we had an argument earlier that day." "Okay, but nobody knew what the argument was about," She responded.

"No Momma T they didn't, they were just speculating like messy bitches do and went running they mouth about shit they didn't know. So now I'm a little upset with Justice. Because I'm like why did you tell her anything about what was going on in my house. Because of ya'll little conversation? You got niggas thinking I was the cause, me, his wife. *'They are saying I killed him.'* *I told* *him.* All he could do was look confused as to why his mother would go running her mouth."

"Well you know he didn't know any better," "Yeah I know but at the time it was hurtful and I was hurting. He knew how his mother was. Shit she was like that his whole damn life. Twisting and turning shit around. So I felt like he helped her make me look bad. I explained it to him. He understood where I was coming from after the fact." I explained. "But you said that at the time you thought it was

51

because of Tane' being nosy, "she questioned.

"Yeah I did," I replied. "Until last year when I was told that it was Kia who called up north and made the comment that I must feel real bad knowing I was the cause."

"Why would she say something so hurtful? Why? Because of the argument you said ya'll had? I know ya'll had worse fights than that. I hope you ain't go blaming yourself."
I really don't know how I was looking on the outside but my insides were wrecked. Benz said when she got there I was in the fetal position on my kitchen floor. The pain she saw was shocking. She said she didn't know what to do; no words could change the situation. I'm just glad she got there when she did. With so many on lookers you would think someone would've stopped me from snatching myself bald.

What girl? Momma T interjected. Didn't that hurt?

Momma T honestly I don't even remember doing it. The pain I was in numbed me from the pain I should have been feeling. Shit I just found out about. I've been upset with losing my hair for years and Benz finally said to me *"you don't remember do you? Why do you think it was so hard to come around you?"*

"Wow, I'm so sorry," she continued "You said I would be crying. I couldn't even begin to imagine just how much pain you were in. I can hear it a thousand times but no one will ever know the feeling first hand like you. I have to say you are very strong. Just to be able to tell me all of this. Tells me that you have more strength than you give yourself credit for."

Chapter 4

The dial on the clock of life stopped ticking at 7:58 on

August 1, 2006.

Since then I have been just living

The Ceramic Doll

As the casket rolled by my heart grew heavy and the tears poured thinking to myself that's my husband. I just stared at the moving box while they rolled him into the room and stopped, locked the wheels in place and opened the hood to the bed his physical will now call home. Every emotion known to man was felt and none felt good.

Looking at Sean was hurtful here I am in pain and he's resting like sleeping beauty all at peace and waiting for a kiss to wake him up. If only it was that simple. Why is it I have to say goodbye when I wasn't the one to leave. I want to just hug him and tell him 'baby get up you know how long you've been sleeping?'

But the reality is I can't all I can do is stare at his lifeless body and feel the coldness with each touch. He can't feel my kisses or warm hand holding his, or hear the pain of each heart beat or see the tears stream down my face. I'm in pain because his gain was my loss.

"For days after my husband passed I wasn't sleeping and didn't care to eat. I was just moving because shit I had too. But what kept trippin me out was the fact that Candice someone who I was told didn't care for me was the one who went through it with me. She was there and I didn't know why. All I kept saying to myself was; *what is this bitch getting out of seeing me in so much pain?*"

"I appreciated it so I left it alone, yeah I knew I was going to speak on it, I just didn't know when. Besides that, Kia's ass was doing her own mourning. So she felt like she couldn't come around because not seeing him was too much for her." "Well who lost the husband you or her?" inserted Momma T. "You would have thought hers the way she was acting. I replied"

"It was a week after my husband passed away. Candice, her sister-in-law and I were at Applebee's and regardless of my circumstance; I just had to know why she was being so good to me. Me, the chic that 'Candice and the pussycats' couldn't stand. So while we were waiting on our food. I told her I needed to ask her something on some real grown woman shit.

Candice said all cool and friendly like; *'what's up Storm?'* So I asked Candice; *'what are you getting out of seeing me like this? You've been staying up all night with me, checking up on me and being there more than Kia who I thought was my road dog. Why? When you don't even like me.'* *'Storm, why you think that?'* *'I was always told that you didn't care to be around me and my friends.'* Candice replied.

'Well, I only kept my distance because Kia told me that ya'll didn't care for me. Storm she said that, so did she tell you all the shit she used to say about you. How you were

nothing but a stuck up show off, you didn't feed your kids,
you only favored your daughter and that you used to make
comments about us. The list just went on and on.' Candice
continued.

"As I sat there listening I was hurting on the inside; but
pissed more than anything. *'That bitch'* was all I could
think. *'Candice listen,' I continued, 'honestly the only time*
I had comments was when she brought back ya'll bullshit. I
don't know ya'll to talk about you; so how can I have
something to say about your personal shit unless it was fed
to me. That's why I had to ask you about that. The crazy
shit is; she knew I was going to ask you. I told her I was
going to ask.' That's when Kia was revealed to be the fake
bill she was; at least to me she was.

I'm thinking; *'Wow, that snake ass bitch really was*
fucked up for that.' The whole time I'm purposely putting

them in a hatin bird category when she was a true hatin bird from Brooklyn. So here I am trippin saying my husband warned me and I didn't listen. So it must've been something trifling she did because he don't think bad about many; but Kia for some reason he said was no good.

Now me and Candice choppin' it up like wow so she had everybody thinking bullshit while she was rocking on both sides of the fence. I told Kia that whenever I have the opportunity I was going to check them on their side bar comments so why would she even play it like that. So now not only do I not have my partner for life around; I have snakes hissing in my yard.

To think I was really treating her like she was a sister of mine. Phony ass bill. I'm not going to front and act like that shit didn't hurt, it did and I was. For her to talk bad about me was one thing, but she was talking shit about me, my kids, and 'my husband. Like I was some fucked up parent and a slave to my master type shit." I was baffled.

" There's more Momma T. I later called Jason and told him that we needed to have a talk face to face. He was like '*cool cuzzo.*' Now I'm telling Jason about me and Candice conversation bringing him up to speed and shit and he couldn't make sense of it either. '*Man cuzzo she really said some fucked up shit.*' is all he could say. He was just as stunned as I was.

'*It's fucked up of your wife to be on some bullshit like that.*' Is all I could say to break the awkward silence. '*I did shit for her that you don't even know about. And you repay my kindness by assassinating my character. She honestly needs to see someone about that shit, take some pills, and lay on somebody couch. Something.*' '*Wow Storm, I'm sorry. I don't even know what to say about that. I'll talk to her though.*' said Jason.

It's pretty evident what goes down next. You get a whole lot of well she said this and she didn't tell you she said that; meanwhile I'm saying *Kia you were the narrator that plot was yours.*

Ultimately I became the bad guy because I was the only real one in the equation. No one could understand that I wasn't being messy. I just lost the only one who had my back for sure, so of course I needed to see who was who and what was what. It just wasn't a convenient time for them.

'I can understand that.' Momma T replied

Things were definitely different after that. Kia and I were now just cool while me and Candice started really becoming friends. Kia of course did not like that so eventually she started up some more drama. Kia just couldn't leave well enough alone, she was so unhappy with herself that she purposely plotted evil and waited in the cut for it to unravel.

It wasn't too much longer after the funeral that things changed. Was I prepared for it? No. Was I warned about it? Yes. During your darkest moment is when you see the true colors peeking out from behind the shadows that were once your loved ones and friends.

You're already down and they try to put you under the ground. I already told you that after the incident with Kia I started stepping back, but I stayed around just enough for the kids to keep in contact with their family. Shit they already had to deal with the loss of their father; I didn't want them to feel completely isolated. Then there's times when you have to know when to walk away. And that time came when the matters of respect no longer seemed to be existing."

Chapter 5

Like a Lady

When the friend you confide in becomes your enemy you

have no choice but to hold it in & walk silently away. You

think loud but your voice makes no sound. Who can you

trust now? Every word ever said was formed against you.

So our relationship never prospered. I just turned around

and exited like a lady. Silent!

"Every day secretly for the first six months I went to the cemetery. And every day I would be more hurt and even more mad. I couldn't sleep because the minute I closed my eyes I knew I would wake up to my reality. So for them same six months I went nonstop with three hours minimum sleep. I napped in spurts but never in the house. I just couldn't sleep. I just stared at the walls. Stared at his clothes. Stared at his empty spot through the mirror. I just stared.

I couldn't keep going to Wally World every night so eventually I started going to the club. That was the vice I needed to fill the hours at night alone. Going to the club was a perfect fit. And so that became my schedule. Come home. Get the kids ready for school. Go to work. Travel home. Go to the cemetery. Go home. Do homework with the kids. Fix dinner. Get them ready for bed and then head to the club."

"Every day, child?" asked Momma T. "Yes Ma'am. Six days a week. And on Sunday I'll get in before the kids get up. Shit, shower and shave. Go to church; then to the cemetery, then to the store and pick up dinner. Cook; get school clothes ready. Get them down and then stay up that night folding laundry or hit the club. I carried that on for about seven months. Keeping myself busy helped me pass the time. The busier I kept; meant the less time I had to face my pain. The reality of being alone."

"You must have run yourself sick. Nobody can do that much running and not collapse." Coaxed Momma T.

"Well I did just that and more. Being that I wasn't eating or sleeping like I should. My body internally started shutting down. I could no longer fit any of my clothes due to the rapid weight loss. My white blood count was extremely low. Low enough for a Urinary Tract Infection to infect my whole uterus.

Shit I was in pain with that for two weeks before it became unbearable. I was in so much pain it felt like my insides wanted to drop right out. I had numbed myself from feeling to the point that I didn't even know I was actually sick and not just heartbroken. The Doctor said my whole body was in a depressive state. That I was clinically depressed and they wanted to medicate me." I paused after saying that... waited for a response. None. So I continued.

"So now I'm to the point when I had to tell myself to slow the fuck down. I don't want to allow myself to feel pain. So why the hell would I want to volunteer myself to be doped up like a zombie. Walking around with a medicated grin. Miss me with that bullshit. They thought I was coming back for that appointment. I'm good. I just slowed things down a little. Enough to put me in a coma for the night and to keep me from crashing again. You still

there Momma T?" "Yes, baby, I'm still here."

Now here comes the

setback.

Chapter 6

"It was the weekend of my husbands' birthday. Me and Benz were going to celebrate it at The Velvet Room. Right before we were leaving out Jason called and said that he haven't spoken to me in a while wished me a "*Happy Birthday in my husbands' place*" and asked what I was getting into. After I said I was headed to the club to celebrate my husbands' birthday he said cool we all going to come through. Well it turned out that He was the only one that showed up.

He got all the way to the club and had to turn back around cause he didn't have the right shoes on. So he was like go ahead cuzzo get right I'll be back. You just get right. At first I didn't think anything of his comment. After all he was my husbands' people. So I'm like aight cool. Hit me when you get back and I'll come back to the door.

Now the whole time at the club he just kept hovering

over me. Buying me drink after drink. All the while coaching me to just get right. He wouldn't let me dance with anyone. But kept trying to dance with me. Eventually I pulled Benz to the side and was like yo; what the fuck is this nigga doing?

She was like what are you talking about? He just wants to make sure you have fun Storm. Nah, he being a little too extra with it. C'mon let's go to the bathroom. As soon as I got in there I poured the drink out. And as the drinks came I just kept dumping them into the flower pot near the dance floor."

"Storm don't tell me that he made a pass at you."

"Yeah Momma T he did. That was the straw that broke the camels' back. I couldn't even believe it. Here I am hurting and trying to enjoy my husbands' day without him and he would dare disrespect me in such a way. Through tears he can apologize for my loss yet tell me he knows I have needs, and how he used to tell my husband that I was a good woman. That he shouldn't be so jealous because he saw that I was loyal. I was beyond pissed yet I still was thinking about his bitch's wellbeing and how messy things would be.

For the kids and all involved. That was just a bad position period. I could just imagine how that would have played out. Me the widow who is miserable trying to wreak havoc on everyone else's lives because mine was unhappy. But that; that right there was my pink slip. I could no longer be around her or anyone for that matter and just not say anything. So I stepped away.

On top of dealing with the messy bullshit with most of the wives. I now have to worry about which one of their husbands are daydream fucking me. A group of people that were a comfort are now a hazmat sign reading caution.

I'm being judged by the jury of conniving bitches and preyed upon by the trifling disrespectful bastards. I'm trying to get by day by day and they trying to get over in every way. The situation just became too uncomfortable. I'm now the victim with no voice because it's too much for them to believe that the advances were one sided." I shook my head at the thoughts all over again.

"Okay so now I try rocking them to sleep to ease them silly ass bitches minds. I just started pretending. Pretending to be having so much fun with niggas that I would meet that instead of putting their minds to ease. I became everything in the book but Storm, Sean's widow. And the niggas they just got more aggressive with it.

It didn't matter who I was with or where I was they made it their business to make it known that they were watching and interested.

I figured maybe if I had a nigga. They'll fucking by a vowel and catch a clue. No those niggas is still till this day begging; asking me if I would tell. Bottom line is that I didn't want yo ass while he was alive. Why would I want your asses now?" I hoped she understood my description.

So tell me Momma T said did Kia ever find out? Eventually it came out over some bullshit universal text message about her choosing to keep me in her life. Seeing it hit a nerve and bottom line Jason was forced to tell on himself. At first she was all apologetic and understanding of why I removed myself. But that only lasted minutes. I still laugh at the words she said; *"I'm not going to let no bitch with a rep like yours rain on my parade. I'm just now starting to shine. You were the bitch then; and now I'm the*

bitch now". I just looked at the text and said to myself wow

my dude for real. That's what it was about.

"Wow," said Momma T. "that is something else. For

anyone to deal with all of that. More power to you. You

could have easily snuck around with clearly anyone of

them that you chose. And instead of them embracing your

loyalty they threw stones. The saying goes "You think the

way you are". Honey you didn't need them bitches. They

shit was damaged before you became a widow. You were

just a convenient blame."

Chapter 7

One more chance!

In life so many things can be taken for granted. Many of us

can daily, really not reflect on the joys of having the things

and people we have. We either hold back or strike back.

And get too scared of being on the median. Until that one

day you can't any more. Suddenly you get smacked with

the reality that when it's over it's really over.

Yes people, "till' death do you part." Really means you do

part. All lines of communication are completely cut off.

The plug wasn't just pulled. The wires were cut in half.

Your heart feels like the drop ride at Six Flags. You

swallow a lot of your tears and hide the pain from the un-

heard cries.

To be able to hear them speak your name.

Or the chance to say I love you more than you'll ever

know. And see them smile and respond I love you too.

Now all you have is fading memories and wishes of just

five minutes.

"Lord please just five minutes, that's all I ask." Then that

last tear in your throat causes real tears to form. You're

missing them and it hurts. But you're holding the tears back

because you're mad. That hole in your chest feels like the

weight of a bullet proof vest. Yet pushing through the pain

is that one wish for things to be back the same. After death

all anyone ever dreams about is if they had

One more chance!

How do you talk about pain and not have tears forming in your eyes. The memories alone leave knots in your throat. Yeah people will ask how you are; but it's never genuinely meant for conversation. There are times when talking about it is soup for the soul.

Then there are those times when talking about it brings a commodity of emotions. How do you really talk about it? Who the hell wants to be judged by another's action? I can only go off the outcome and the outcome doesn't coincide with anything I know.

Hi my name is Storm; I'm a widow with four kids. My life came spiraling down because I was an emotional wreck after my husband passed away. How you ask? He attempted to commit suicide and succeeded. Yeah that sounds like a great opening when you've come to a point when you're finally ready to move on. Here you are trying to be comfortable with opening your heart and scared of being judged by your past. Just the mere fact that the answers you do have are not for the questions that are being asked.

So do you go on with life hiding from the truth? Do you talk about it with hopes of no judgments' and complete understanding? All the things that you long for and miss; can you get that back. Is it at all possible or will I be a widow for the rest of my life? Well hiding from the truth has been getting me by on the outside, that's the only lie I have been able to tell over and over. It's so easy to say that He's been killed; than to say He killed himself.

Even though it hurts like hell to want to talk about what the truth is. I know I need to face the harsh reality that just maybe it wasn't an accident and it was just too late for him stop. The fact that I will never know why bothers the shit out me. Guess that's why no one knows the truth; and the answers he took right along with him.

"Storm this may sound like a stupid question. But were there really no signs of trouble?" "Well Momma T that's one thing my husband always said. There's no such thing as a stupid question, you're only stupid if you don't ask. But to answer your question…

The only sign that was overlooked was when we had the conversation about him feeling like he was going to die. Other than the argument we had there was nothing. My brother and I go over the same questions. There was really nothing. And if there was he hid it very well. I wrote him a letter stating all of that." "You wrote who a letter?" "Sean, I wrote it and dropped it in the hole with him." I said flatly.

Dearest Sean,

Even though your eyes will never see this letter, I felt it was time to let go of all that I've been holding inside. I have over the months forgiving you somewhat and with time I'll be able to move past the hurt. But one thing that will never change is the memories. Guess the saying is true; one moment can bring you a lifetime of pain..................

I try to make sense of it every day; was there something that I missed? Could I have been able to prevent him from leaving the world that day? Were you depressed? Did you feel overwhelmed? Did someone threaten you? Was there another woman? What the fuck was it? It's going on two years now and I still ask that one question. What the fuck was it? What could have possibly been going on that you felt there was no way out but to checkout. To actually be that damn selfish. What about Our kids? Me? Your

parents? All the people that was going to be affected by
that.

How do you just walk away and not give any
answers. How do you leave like that? I always felt that
there was nothing that would come between us. Nothing
that we couldn't handle. We were a team. We had a plan
and you broke that. You broke up our home. Our hearts
and crushed our souls. You left me to answer questions that
I didn't have the answers to.

As much as I love you part of me hate you for that. I
look at our kids and I hurt for the years to come. You
robbed them of their natural born right to grow up with a
father. You gave them pain that will be with them for the
rest of their life. But did you think of that, did you think of
what kind of impact that would have on them?

As they watch other kids with their dad and all they can
do is think about wanting theirs back.

Justice I can't really say, the day he was forced to leave
was the last time we had any real contact for a long time.
Tane even had the nerve to tell me that if she caught us
communicating she'd file harassment charges against me.
All the while probably filling his head with the many
reasons why he don't hear from your side of the family.

Even though I can't change her I told Justice that he
would always have a home with me and as much as I want
him with me I have to respect the fact that she is his mother
and regardless to how fucked up she may be he has to let
her be a mother to him and respect her just the same. Sad
part is He lost a father and contact with us on the same day
and it didn't have to ever be that way. You was his life
coach, he needed you.

Malik, poor thing wouldn't let me out of his sight for months. He just kept worrying and being scared all the time. I had to pep talk with him just so I can go to the store. He would always just sit at the window waiting for my return. King he's more like me, tough on the outside with a hanging heart on the inside.

Nyima she cried for you for weeks. Every time she saw a van that resembled yours she would cry. I had to ask the neighbor to park his van elsewhere cause she would just sit by the patio door and yell her heart out, she just cried.

The 1st time taking her to your burial site. Was the hardest thing ever. For a mother to not be able to console her own child is heart breaking. When it was time to go she kicked and screamed all the way to the car. She just wouldn't stop yelling for her daddy, I want my daddy; I *want to stay here with my daddy. And there was nothing that I nor her brothers or your cousin could do to comfort her.*

She yelled herself into a deep sleep. Even though I have talked with her about death and why she can't see you anymore, she still asks for you. Wanting to know when is her daddy coming back?

Do you know how that feels? Did you factor that into the equation? When you walked away you took so much with you. More than what the heart can bear. It hurts that you walked away but it hurts more because you left with no answers.

Hurting Soul...

Chapter 8

I just really had to sit back and look at my picture I didn't

like it so I turned the channel

I was living, but I was living in   another realm. Somewhat like a mannequin on display. Everybody sees it dressed to the nines with accessories and smile. Being in the midst of small to large crowds daily. Yet; no one ever recognizes its emptiness. The wrong amount of pressure put against it will cause it to collapse into pieces. That's me.

The physical awareness that life around me was still moving along with the same time that was passing me by. The emptiness the hurt was causing was too much to face. So I started filling that hole with whatever numbed the pain for that time. I lost a husband, son, extended family, close friends, touch with reality, and the sensation of feeling good from within.

The will to acknowledge love. No matter how much I

stuffed that hole. Nothing right will ever be right because I wasn't in a place to accept all things good.

Can you see the pain in my eyes? Dismiss my actions and listen to my heart. I'm hurting. Spending my loneliest times holding back the tears. The rest of the time smiling while hurting inside. Loving is so hard now, it's like I did it and I was left stuck on that shit. I gave a piece of me and got an empty room in return.

For where my heart once resided is now a vacant lot. Heart be hurting so much you get a headache from the thoughts. That's one of the many side effects of a broken heart. You get stuck, you go numb, you freeze hard and then you never stop fighting. You suffer something like a chemical imbalance.

Everything is all off track and anyone is suspect. And

that's only because you feel like you're not going to give someone the opportunity to fuck you over. It's just not going to happen. Period, point blank, end of story. You either going to be all the way in or all the way out; that in between shit was not cutting it. To let my guard down and you don't protect it like you on sloman shields payroll, can't risk it.

"Some people say that I'm too hard and talk like a dude, cool! Call me the pit bull. Shit call me whatever you like but it won't be any ones fool. Bet that!"

"Girl you're a mess." She laughed. "Nah momma T, when you deal with the many trifling, ignorant mother fuckers I've been coming across. You just want to throw your hands up and ask; did I get mixed in with the dummies on purpose. Was I supposed to be the one to put these niggas in they place and let them know that not every song is about them."

"But Storm, not everyone is like that. There are some good guys left." Said Momma T. "Yeah that's true and all, but am I going to risk the bullshit to find out. Hell Nah. I did. I know how the book ends."

You know Momma T; I didn't start packing his clothes until about a year after he passed. Even then it was a forced decision. Up till that point everything was kept in its original state. I used to wear his robe to bed; I used to brush my teeth with his toothbrush, spray his cologne on an article of his and just sit there sniffing his scent. His laundry was preserved in a plastic bag and I would sometimes smell his socks just to remember how we used to joke about his toe funk.

I missed all the little things that people take for granted. So going through the same amount of pain and anguish again is not even an option.

"So what, you going to be dealing with your own kind?" she injected. "Momma T, I'm so straight on that. I'm just saying. I'm choosing to stay single. It's the safest route when there's heavy traffic."

"When I make a decision it's not just about me. I have to base it off of what kind of affect it would have on my kids. So I can't afford to do the whole trial and error thing. Nope I have kids to live for. They already don't have one parent. I look at niggas as a health hazard. A death certificate waiting to be signed.

I'm not trying to be a GCASH candidate for nobody. So to be with me is to be all the in or all the way out."

"I guess I understand," she continued. "Things were different for me. In my days a man knew what it took to court a woman." "Yeah," I responded "but then I know

97

ya'll had your share of the I'm too fly to be with one type of guy." "Well my late Charles was a ladies' man. But he also knew what that kind of temptation was going to get him. So I had a smart ladies man." concluded Momma T. "Well momma T I'm going to let you get some rest as well as myself. Talk to you same time tomorrow." "Goodnight Storm."

"Goodnight!"

Chapter 9

Dear Friend,

There were many days and nights

That I wanted to call upon you for help.......

The Next Night: "How can I be getting punished so badly, what the fuck did I ever do to anybody that would get me dealt a hand like this. Worst of all I'm mad at myself for allowing things to get so bad. It's almost like tug a war. On the left side I have all the people I have to pay money to every month."

"They don't care if you don't have it. You late, you pay more. Then on the right side you have your kids. You can't deny them. So where does that leave you. Between a rock and a hard place. It's not that you want to be late you have no choice. Certain situations and circumstances forces you to take from one spot and put to another. So you suffer in silence as your being tugged in two different directions."

"Isn't that the truth. I've had my share of not knowing where the next meal was coming from. It's one thing to just have you to worry about yourself. I can only imagine what it's like to carry three kids along the struggle. But I still say your stronger than most. Not many women can go through as much as you did and still stand. But go on baby." I must admit, talking to Momma T was comforting.

"When you go from having it all too slowly waking up to the reality of having nothing. Falling short of having the mere basic necessities. You just find yourself angry. Angry about the situation, angry about why the situation is even taking place, and angry at the individual who was supposed to help prevent it. In this case it's Sean."

"One day I had to tell my brother he really didn't understand. Everybody acts like I'm the one who was supposed to be calling around the world to see how their doing when I'm the one who sleeps alone at night. And that's if I even sleep. But no; everyone wants to talk about how I'm not acting the way they feel a widow should act.

But tell me how is it a widow should be. You're struggling for understanding, strength, identity, support and the ability to just move without hurting."

"Sis!" – He tried to insert. But I stopped him.

"No let me finish I been wanting to vent this shit out for the longest. I was just waiting for someone to actually say to me that the reason people don't call or come see about his kids or wife is because of me, the widow. The person who lost their other half don't reach out to ya'll.

Yeah everybody had a loss that day but no one suffered from it like me and at the end of the day each of you have someone to turn to. I shared a bed *with him for eleven years and now when I lay down and turn to my right all I see is emptiness. That's all I feel and that's all I see. And none of ya'll can tell me how that feels. Having your insides frozen and numb. While swallowing a knot in your throat.*

The faintest beat of your heart is like a pain in your chest. Grasping for air while you pray for strength and to make it to see another day.'"

"So what did he say?" "He apologized and said he didn't know. That I was absolutely right and he was going to make it his business to stay in our lives the way he knew Sean would have if the shoe was on the other foot. We really became tight after that conversation. Of course people have a problem with that. They so programmed into thinking the worst that they can't see at the end of the day its' about the kids."

"Yeah well you know Storm if that's all their women ever worry about when it comes to you; then I would let them drive themselves sick with mental anguish."

Sometimes I have to catch myself.

Swallow them words and erase the thought!

"Not being able to provide for my kids the way they were used to is the hardest part of healing. I get so frustrated at not being able to do just the basics that it eats my insides. You know that nervous stress pain. Where every moment feels like a panic attack waiting to happen.

The will I be able to syndrome. Heart be pounding so fast with anguish that you have to apply pressure to the spot just to slow it down. On top of that you have the lil innocent bystanders looking at you with eyes of confusion.

How do you tell your kids no because your too proud to tell them you can't afford it and the fuck dudes that call themselves your Uncles think I'm going to fuck them for a favor. Yeah shit really changes when become a widow. You go from being a member of the wives club to the president of the I'll fuck your husband committee. With all this dick in Georgia they think I'm desperate enough to stoop lower than a whore. Talk about bitches turning they back.

With Sean gone things really got rough, I sometimes had to force myself to flirt with a few of them fuck dudes just to get money for bills. Then it turned into me really having to gas a few individuals' heads up to the fullest. Shit if these lame ass niggas thought for one second that they was going to hit it cause they gave up some grocery money then let the mind games begin. Especially Candice's dude because that nigga just thought he was a pussy pleaser for real. Little did they know my stomach churned with every word uttered.

Man when I think back to how things were before Sean passed I just get a pit full of rage boiling inside me. *Like nigga you left me to deal with this bullshit by myself.* I moved my ass all the way from NY to be abandoned with the rats and roaches from NY, ain't that some shit.

The funny thing is even if I needed to call them. I wouldn't. Sometimes I have to catch myself, swallow those words and erase the thought. This one fucked up email put a cease to that. The moment I laid eyes on that email was the last time I asked anyone that was supposed to be someone for shit. Matter of fact I remember exactly what it said.

He was like *we had you included automatically with our paper we was going to look out just cause, but then all that nonsense that went on after son passed was crazy, we made a pact not to give up no bread on the strength of what went on. I was tight cause all we wanted to do was record we didn't want to keep the equipment! And now for you to ask for bread seem like some bullshit only because you act like everything is all good...I mean you never even spoke on it! I mean don't get it twisted Storm I love you and the kids*

on another level that's why I gave you that shortbread but

now I have to get something out the deal. If I'm going to

even think about giving up anything anymore! You mad

smart, you still young, still look good I don't want to feel no

kind of way, I want to fuck with you on a lot a things! But

can I trust u? All I could do was stare at the screen and

think what the fuck (excuse my French) is that supposed to

mean

Okay let me get this straight. Because you learned after experiencing an event which was traumatizing for anyone that your so called "family" was being a conniving bitch behind your back for months on end. That made you the enemy." Stated Momma T.

"So, being fake would have been rewarded. Then what did he mean by if he was going to give you anymore he would have to be getting something in return. What? A Thank you. The kids and I appreciate you. What equipment was he talking about asked Momma T.

He was referring to the studio equipment my husband purchased for his business ventures in management. So if the equipment was your husbands. Momma T interjected; why do you owe anyone an explanation. "You know we say nothing ceases to amaze us but this honey has me amazed. I'm really in awe at the actions that took place. What about your family?

Well Momma T you realize years later that things were always just a step away from being fucked up, I know many niggaz that don't have a room forced to sleep on some ones couch or floor because those that can spare have no heart and the ones with heart have barely enough to share.

yet you dare to make a boy scout honor to purposely turn your back, but you know what its' cool cause see I'm the type of bitch that will respect your wishes and still wish you well because see at the end of the day it's about the kids and even though isolation is a struggle I rather go at it alone then to call upon so called family. It stings more than anything that you force your mouth to stay closed because you rather miss six meals so you don't sound like your begging for one.

Yes people, your so called loved ones have the nerve to call it begging. No it's never to your face but from personal experience I know it to be true. I say there should be no reason why someone you would consider family or your neighbor for that matter be in need and you not offer. Yet all these church going spiritual souls can be so cold.

That's one thing about me I'm honest with my kids and I don't sugar coat shit because at the end of the day I'm not guaranteed to be here and I refuse to let them be dependent upon anyone or anything. I explain to them about the genuineness of peoples concerns.

Above all the bullshit we have one thing greater and that's knowing the true meaning of Love because when that one moment is gone there is no chance to do things right. We love and give genuinely to each other, women, children & family without expectations. After all isn't that the Godly way. I wrote a letter to them folks too.

Okay let me strap my seatbelt on because knowing you it's tactfully said and well put. One of those if it don't apply let it fly moments.

Greetings: Ha-Satan,

CC: Lucifer,

CC: Shaitan, Iblis

The truth! So people want the truth. Lets' just see how much of the truth can one handle. Now someone out there will be feeling some kind of way. different strokes for different folks and if the shoe fit well then wear it well. To be more blunt about the shit , I ask who the fuck is you?

So the marked beast wants to sit back and talk about how I shitted on them, how my attitude is so fucked up towards them, how I don't look out for them. Well you know what my heart learned to say… fuck you and your conflicted feelings.

It's funny how I'm a good friend but you better watch her around your man, or I'm the go to girl when shit is rough and you need something, but I'm *'sometimey'* if I'm not able to help. Well if I'm such a good friend from the heart then these issues wouldn't come up behind my back and the last time I checked the Lord did bless me with three children so yes there will definitely be times when I am forced to say no because I have to tell them yes. So get over yourselves not every song is about you.

It's crazy how I can open my home and heart. Invade my kids' space; take food and money from their mouths to make shit work out for seven extra ungrateful mother fuckers. To not only destroy what was a lovely home, you fucking stole from me. While I was mourning the loss of my husband you took my kindness for weakness and now you want to point fingers.

How is it a mother fucker can do you wrong, know in their heart they are wrong and were wrong yet still try to make your reaction the main focus of the problem. I can sit here and point many fingers, and say many names. For what? The same way you shitted on me karma will shit on you.

Truth is I've never been the picture of perfection. I've always been a smart mouth bitch and when mixed with anger it's like opening Pandora's Box. I've done things out of anger, acted prematurely because of stupidity and allowed the devil to wreak havoc on my soul out of ignorance.

I've blocked countless blessings for revealing out of anger my good deeds done. By way of heart I'm kind, by way of greed people assume the right to take advantage. Someone once told me that people only deal with me because I have something they need.

I say who's the bigger ass when you act on queue

because your needy ass is back with your hand out. So yes

you call me a liar, hoe, a lame ass nigga, I have issues, I'm

bitter, a sneak and I fell off after my husband passed away.

Wow! the list goes on and on.

I always have someone emailing, texting or posting or

passing the word of what is supposed to be hurtful and

insulting, naturally I get annoyed because their ignorance

makes me think of my acts of kindness and I say to myself

how can someone harbor such hatred yet fake so much

love. Well King and Angels of the bottomless pit I'm far

from naïve but I see that you are of your father and I of

mines.

I am who I am!

Ar-Rahmaan!

Chapter 10

"Hey Momma T"

"Hey baby"

"How was your day today?"

"It was long waiting till ten. Who made up that rule anyway? I've been itching to call."

"Well I guess it was because we always end it off with same time tomorrow."

"C'mon you're doing that suspense thing again. Get to reading I done told you child' you need to write a book."

"The day I was stepping into the fast life I called my bro. You know Seans' best friend."

"Okay, I remember."

"It started off with a sigh. He said it's that bad sis? Well I 'm actually calling because no one knows where I'm at. He automatically knew what I was talking about. He said "you said that would never be an option". I know. Damn sis I knew things were bad but I didn't know shit was that bad. This was like a last resort if anything no resort.

'So it's that bad?' 'Yea Bro it's that bad and my back is up against the wall. You know all I need is one good come up to get shit back on track. 'I'm not going to beat you up about it I know you already did enough of it yourself. You nervous?' 'No. just feels like this shit is getting really crazy.'

'Well where are you? Who you with?' 'Remember home girl who was staying with me till the kids got back.' 'Yeah, I thought she was a quiet church girl. A bubble head.' 'Yeah well I guess those are the ones. Her dude owns a club out here and once a month they have dancers' night. She said it was an upscale club. No touching. No nudity just basically dancing and walking around in sexy lingerie.' 'Alright it don't sound that wild. Only time right?

'You already know.' 'Be safe sis and watch your drink and I'm a call you in the morning.' 'Okay!'

'Okay so how did things go? Momma T asked.' 'Hold on I'm getting to that part.'

'It's 3 O'clock in the morning and I'm pissed. This bitch took my kindness for weakness and fucking tried me. I opened my home to her in a time of need and she fucking tried me. So I called my mother because not only was I pissed but I was hurting. I was hurting because I knew that if I took the actions I was feeling I would have been locked up. Something I damn sure couldn't afford at the time. Being too far to be bailed out.

My mother answered the phone she sound like she was sleeping, so I told her I was sorry to have woken her but I just didn't have anybody else to call.' 'What's wrong my mother asked?' 'Well you know how I joke about getting on the pole every night.' 'Yea, but You know you have more options than that. Where are you?' 'Well I came to NC to do just that and this bitch tried to have me on some players club shit. She tried me, I snarled. I just want to whoop her ass so bad but I know I'm too far from home.' 'You don't need to be getting yourself locked up way out there, just make it home and cut her loose.'

'She said what I needed to hear at the time, but in my heart I was feeling like I wanted to wrap my hands around her neck and choke the shit out of her. I mean she really thought I was that damn simp.

The next morning my brother called.' 'That's Seans' Best friend right? Yes Momma T him.' 'Okay continue baby.'
Hey Sis, man brother I interjected this bitch tried me.

What? What happened? I thought shit was supposed to be cool. Start from the beginning. Alright. Well you know how no one but us knew I was supposed to be there, at least that's what I thought. Well things were cool till we got to the club. So we get there and right off the rip the damn bouncer was like so what up ATL you going to show them how it's done as he's talking she on some slick sly shit trying to shh him. So I was like nah where u get your info from I'm from Arkansas and from that point on it was bullshit after bullshit. Passed the doors you walk into what looks like class I thought okay not bad at all.

I went with a plan and I was going to stick and move just like planned. I signed up paid my little forty cent then went to what was considered a dressing room. I was a bit pissed it was like we were in a bus station, bags, rags, bitches and niggas. A musical chair set up and one crowded ass mirror and now here her silly ass go with the comforting stripper talk as I'm getting dressed. So I roll my blunt up and I'm on some okay I'm here let's do this type shit. Head downstairs to the so called elegance and it was like walking into what is actually three steps below The Cave, the fucking stage she talked about was just a pole right in the middle of the dance floor....... Talk about being heated. I just couldn't believe I let myself get caught up in the hype. So now I'm walking around peeping the scenery of broke niggas to hungry bitch ratio and I'm saying wow ain't this some shit.

Chilling in the cut this bitch come talking about I got someone you can practice on, what the fuck you mean practice nah what you can do is get me a drink since I can't fucking smoke. Security in the club kept throwing slick hints my way but wouldn't say shit when she came back around us.

Asking me how I know the bitch and how I don't even look like I would be caught dancing at a spot like this, that she haven't been there in a minute but she usually brings more than one girl....... More than one girl I thought, wow! Okay, this bitch is playing me. So when her ass got back with my drink I was like you know what I'm good. This shit is too nasty for me.

So she start going on saying what about the money, think about the kids. I looked at the stupid broad and said just be ready when I'm done. After that I went to go change and what do I walk in on, her and her dude arguing about why I wasn't dancing, they so damn caught up they didn't even notice me standing there.

'Wow Sis are you serious?' Brother the turning point was when the damn bitch brought me an open bottle of water talking about I thought you were thirsty. I look at the shit and said I didn't fucking say I was thirsty I told you to be ready, so she tried to walk off like she had a fucking tude and shit. I grabbed her by the arm and was like look I give you your props for getting me down here but bitch if we don't walk out the door now I'm going to forget the cops are outside. So fuck finding your nigga and walk your ass to the door now.

Man shawty do you know the minute we walked out the door her phone started going off and whoever it was they wanted to know what happened and she was like things didn't go as planned.'

'Damn sis I'm glad you didn't drink that shit you probably would've been all fucked up not remembering shit.'

'Wow, Momma T interjected I'll tell you one thing.

Those footprints are clearly in the sand when you walk. Because no matter what the Devil tried to do to you. That path straightens right back out. And coupled with that you have brains. If you would've been a dummy, well let's just be thankful you're not. Because we've all seen the players club.

As we chuckled at the thought Momma T said girl finish, this is getting good. I know I may sound like a broken record but I tell you, you should write a book child.' 'Yeah it would be a good read I stated.'

So I step outside and she chillin talking to my neighbor. I take a seat on the steps and exchange a few hellos with my neighbor. Then she asks how my trip was. So I'm like not what I expected it to be; but I'm cool. So here this bitch go. She would have came up if she didn't back out. So I'm like "What Bitch?" Then she tried to change it up a bit and say. The money was there you just had to go get it. So I was like "so why the fuck you ain't go get it. If the money was there why the fuck you ain't get it.

This bitch going to say all prissy and shit "Oh that's not for me". I can't do that. I just throw parties. Oh, but you can nominate me. When you didn't have shit I gave you a roof no questions but you want to offer me that in return. Like you were doing me some kind of favor. I will fuck yo ass up. Man shawty the only thing saving you is yo kids right now. You knew that shit when we left. I said I was going to fuck yo ass up when I got back. But you got smart and picked up your kids along the way. But being that you want to get fly. When I wake up I don't want to see yo ass. Bitch I mean that shit let me see you. All I need is one glimpse.

"Well was she gone?"

"Yeah she was gone but I guess she either thought I needed to calm down or she had to con the next person first cause she damn sure forgot to take her shit with her. Then later on that night the silly hoe send me a damn text about going to the club with her. I'm looking at the text thinking; what the fuck, like shawty you tried me. No matter how you try to pretend that shit wasn't the way I felt it. You tried me."

"So what did you say to her?"

"Nothing the only message I needed to see was her asking if she could come get her stuff and better had been before the kids got back or it wouldn't have been anything for her to get. Crazy shit is all her peoples started dropping dime on her after the fact. Even her own nigga called himself apologizing for how things went down because he thought I knew what her hustle was."

"Wow some hustle. But Storm I bet she thinks twice now about a mark."

"Yeah but it took baiting me to learn that lesson."

Chapter 11

Just when you think you're alone, He sends one of his

Angels to be the ear for a searching soul!

Storm Momma T said: it may not seem like it, but those clouds are just passing through. You've held your head high through every block that you've walked. Passing by many temptations and keeping faith in your heart. You have tackled every adversity. Walking against the storm. You are a wonderful mother and will make someone a proud husband again. Just let yourself feel and stop fearing the feeling.

You know Momma T I've always believed people come into your life for a purpose higher than we know. I also told myself I would never experience the pain of losing to love lost again. For that pain is like a bullet penetrating to the core of your soul. The not so funny thing is I have men call me bitter till this day....

I'm not too sure of when the rain will stop but the storms they'll calm down in time.... It's said that that it takes at least eighteen months to be in a place of acceptance. Do you know how many days, hours, minutes and seconds that is. Now add the feeling of shock that was felt when you first realized something or someone special was lost- gone for good. You there?'

'Yeah I feel you said Momma T.' 'Now just imagine the emptiness, heavy heart and struggle to breathe. When the only thing you can do is beg for God to take the pain away.

I've been fighting to see the other side for 3yrs 9mths and 3dys now and every time I feel like I'm making a break thru the devil sends in his reinforcements and I go back into my bubble where my pain became my comfort. It's pretty sad and I know it's more damaging to hold on than it is to let go, or maybe the anger consumes me and the guilt rides me.......

Whatever it is, it just eats away my happiness and makes me ice cold, I hate that I'm this way yet I'm running out of solutions for fixing me,....

I sleep all day, stay up all night, shop with no purpose, go out just to kill time, pretend to not care, love or feel any emotion. I surround myself with children because I rather babysit than to relate. I ended up here because I never dealt I just coped. I never let go I just mastered the artistry of hiding the story behind the eyes.... Some may think it's pretty pathetic and sad but for others like myself it's a safe haven, a hideaway.

Momma t there are so many moments I catch myself looking at my children, daydreaming about all the events and special moments they have ahead and it saddens me inside. Just knowing that every birthday wish made is that one wish that can't be granted. Or the one thing wanted for

Christmas can't be given.

So they still miss him dearly? Momma T interjected. I
mean I know they will always miss him, but is it still as
fresh on their minds as it is with you?

Even though I know they grieve, I grieve for them.
They have their own moments that bring tears to their eyes,
and all I can do is hold them tight, comfort them and
swallow my cries internally. For those are the times my
tears are angry. Then I have the times when the tears are
bitter sweet. Like baby I hope you're seeing this. Look at
our babies. Then that moment leaves me in silence with
heaviness in my stomach because it's now holding my
heart.'

'Wow Storm you sure do have a way with words, my
eyes are crowded with tears because like a spirit speak

through people you speak through your pain. Storm if no one has ever told you, you are a strong woman by many standards. I know it seems like I keep telling you this but God is with you and don't let know one tempt you to believe different.'

'Thanks Momma t, your kind words are really appreciated.' It's my pleasure Storm Momma T stated, everyone needs someone to tell them they are doing good at some point. So have you wrote to Sean since the last letter?'

'Yes I did, You have perfect timing because I actually have it in front of me it was the next page in my journal. But I think we've done enough crying for one night.'

'Girl, Momma T said don't you even tease me like that.' Okay Momma T one more then it's off to bed we both go.' I cleared my throat and began reading.

Hey Baby,

So it's been almost four years and shit has been real crazy. I must say you really left me in a fucked up predicament. So many times over I have played out your moment and my own moment has thoughts in my head.

Then I look at our children and with all my heart I know I could never walk away. I'm too afraid of what this world will do to them. The affect the impact would have. You go your whole life feeling like you can take on the world until your world gets taken from you.

Then you feel like the world will swallow you alive because your security blanket was snatched from your hands. Well that's what you did. You left me so torn that the only emotion I have left is love for children. I tried to love but there's no understanding of missing the dead. You truly are that ghost that you said you would be. Constantly asking what that quiet voice be.

The question that still stings and the bullet still rings. Above all of that my heart still just bleeds. Thanks to DeKalb I had a lie to tell my four crowns but the truth stayed to linger from the report of the examiner and the memories of the those days before you were laid to rest and those doubts was my quest.

I have to admit you were the truth for this shit cause the secrets you went to the grave with it. What a way to breach a contract is how I mostly felt. I didn't realize how much bullshit was blocked being under your wings. Now that the shield is gone it's like the fight don't stop. I guess I can thank you a little.

Because my hand was forced and I had to assume both

titles I'm raising respectful, independent soldiers.

Boo I, well we have sons that are intelligent.. they can greet an adult of both genders and have them off guard with their manner and ways. They cook, clean, and understand how to take care of each other.

There's unity amongst them and its the coolest thing to see. Besides brains and manners they can do twenty pushups without busting a sweat, so I'm doing the discipline thing well too. But I guess you probably knew they were left in good hands.

Your princess is pretty, pretty smart, independent and very precise. A little me with a mouth to match but of course in a respectful expressive way. She can be silly at times and a boss always.

You can say I'm raising men of honor and a proverbs 31

Queen. See boo I think I have the hang of it our children

are smart, soulful, caring, physically fit and talented in

many ways. They are not perfect but they are not

disrespectful mouthy ass unruly kids, yet I manage to do

this without yelling or laying hands. Too bad you robbed

yourself of enjoying these years.

Just a lil Upset

Chapter 12

I have come to learn first hand

By experience that strangers become your closest

Family and family becomes your distant friend

Still the fact is their family so in your heart you love them

all the same. Even though in your pain those were the ones

that never came. From family to friend; from existing to

extinct. In the split of a second as quick as you blink.

Momma T where are you? Ring, ring, ring, ring…… Why isn't she answering? There must be something wrong. Click I hung up the phone for the fifth time. Well I guess I'll try her tomorrow. Nah let me try again.

Hello, hello Momma T! Is that you? 'Well if you give me a chance to talk you would be able to hear that I couldn't pass as nobodies Momma T.' 'Eight? Is that you?' 'Yeah it's me.' 'Man where have you been? I've been trying to contact you for the longest. I even met a nice ol' lady in the process.' 'And I take it the nice ol' lady is Momma T?' 'Yes smart ass.' 'Whatever my number hasn't changed.'

'Well, whatever the mix up was it happened, but the crazy shit is your name is on the caller ID as being a saved contact. Well maybe it was meant for you two to connect.' 'Speaking of Momma T I'm a lil worried about her.'

'Why?' 'Well we've been talking to each other for the past couple of weeks like clockwork at ten on the dot.

Tonight I didn't get an answer. This is not like her, I'm worried.' 'Well then go to her house! I can't, I never got her address and she has a damn Metro.' 'Shit, well when was the last time you called her.' 'Right before you called, I thought that was her when you beeped in.' 'oh, well try again in the morning and if you still don't get her leave a message and wait it out. You know how you be over analyzing.' 'Yeah you right.'

' So other than worrying about Momma T how have you been? I know today's the 1st so I was checking on my friend. I started to pop up but couldn't remember your building number.'

'Wow it's been that long? Some friends we are. I've been good.' 'You sure?' 'Yes. I've Been taking things gracefully.' 'Oh really? So does that mean you're finally putting some weight on?' 'I've been making a conscious effort. It's coming slowly.' 'Yeah that's what your mouth says interjected Eight. I'll have to come by and see for myself. You know how you do; say one thing and be feeling another.

Always trying to be hard like a nigga.' 'I know and believe me I have been trying so please don't make me feel bad about the slow progress. I hear it all the time.' 'Okay you know I'm only asking because I really do care. I just want to make sure you're alright. Alright?'

'Alright I stated!' 'Well I'll call you in the morning to check on you and Storm; the storm is almost over.' 'Thanks Eight. But since we're on the phone can I read to you?

Huh? Well that's what me and Momma Ts' conversations were about. It has been a bit comforting to get the stuff I write out and she has been so encouraging somewhat like you.'

'Well get to reading then, shit I'm just glad you're finally talking about it.'

Hey Up There,

Even though I know your looking down I still feel compelled to write you this letter I'm not too sure if this would be the last one seeming how your departure wasn't a forgetting one but I have a lot of things that just stay bottled up and I'm really wearing myself thin keeping my thoughts to myself yea I know I've said some things in the past and I also know I've sugar coated a whole lot of shit.....

It all started the day you took your life away, I mean accidentally passed away at least that's what they called it. Too bad I read the report so I know that there is some truth to you being the reason even though I want to believe that you would never break a promise, but I was once told promises can be broken.
Boo! You broke your promise. Worst you left me with the guilt. All I think about was your last words to me "if I don't

147

make you completely happy what is my purpose for being here" that phrase just rings in my head only because you made it clear that you were referring to being here as alive and I wonder did you really?

Then I think about what I told you "you're not here to make me happy all the time, no one is happy all day every day and it don't mean it's you, shit I could be upset about anything at any time and it won't have anything to do with you making me happy, then I said I'm done talking about this shit you be tripping for nothing" from the room I heard you open the front door I ran to catch you before you got too far and I said Boo! You turned back to look and I said I Love You!

You just had this blank look on your face...... I wonder what you were thinking at that moment? Did that save you because you came back, but then I was gone and when I got back you were gone..... I think if I would have stayed home or asked you to ride with me could that have made a difference.....if you had your phone would you have attempted to call for help or did you leave it home on purpose.

Why would you call son and tell him you were going to be with your father, clearly stating the one above? I lost four pant sizes in the first week and a total of twenty eight pounds in a sixth month span. I know you saw all the drama with your peoples all I can say was you told me so...........

Quite There!

'That's all Eight asked. Well none the less it was very well expressed. Your words are so poetic and heartfelt.' 'Well its pretty late I interjected and I have to get up in a few hours after all today is the day and I want it to be a peaceful and productive one. No pun intended.' 'Cool Storm I won't push it, it took years just for you to even talk that much. I'll call you later on this evening and remember I'm here no matter what.' 'Awe thanks Eight!'

'No need to thank me I'm doing what I only wish someone would have done for me. Genuinely care enough to just be there without pre or post judgment. I know your pain so being there makes it not easy but welcoming. Sometimes I think about you and the kids and exhale deeply for you for this is just the beginning and the ending seems like a never.' 'tell me about it I interjected.

Well goodnight and I'll talk to you tomorrow.' Okay

Storm make sure you call me the moment you get some

down time.'

Chapter 13

Who the hell is calling me this damn early? Caller ID reading cell phone, GA. Shit leave a message I don't answer if I can't identify. Whoever it is they are persistent. What the hell they keep calling for, finally I answered the phone. Hello! With the you're interrupting me tone. 'Hello can I speak to Storm the caller stated. 'Who should I say is calling? 'This is Stan I'm Mrs. Wilson's son.' 'I'm sorry I don't know a Mrs. Wilson.'

'All her friends called her Momma T'. 'oh, okay. Yeah I know Momma T, but you said called.' 'Yes I did. I noticed that you called her quite a bit yesterday so I figured ya'll were close. I'm sorry to have to be the one to tell you this but; Momma T passed away in her sleep yesterday afternoon.'

'Huh? I knew something was wrong when she didn't answer. Wow, I'm so sorry for your loss.'

'Thanks! Even though it's a sad time, I'm actually happy knowing she won't be going through any more pain.'

'Pain? I didn't know she was sick.' 'Yes, Momma T been sick for some time now. She held on longer than what the doctors anticipated.' 'Well Stan, I appreciate your call and can you please keep me updated on the funeral arrangements, I would love to come and pay my respects. Momma T was really kind to me.' 'Sure Storm I'm pretty sure she wouldn't have it any other way.'

'Hello! Hey Storm Eight stated, How's your day going for you so far?' 'Well it started off with sad news.' 'Oh, why's that?' 'Well I was informed that Momma T, the lady I was telling you about passed away yesterday in her sleep.'

'Wow Storm are you serious? Man. So what did ya'll talk about?' 'I told you. We talked about everything.

Everything I've been wanting to tell anyone but me.' 'How did that work out for you? 'Like I said it did me some good.' 'You sound like it.' 'So would you like for me to come with you to the funeral? I'm actually glad you asked, I've been thinking about asking you all morning.

I just don't know when it is.' 'Well things probably got hectic and it could have slipped their minds. Why don't you pass the number on to me and I'll check into it while you get through the day.' 'You know Eight my heart really appreciates you.

But before we hang up, I think I've finally came to an understanding of how I really got here and why I was so stuck for so long.

A good friend once told me that in order to get over

something it needs to be replaced with something!

They say memories don't live like people do. Well my memories out lived a few. I used to wonder how my heart got here. All my life I've been conditioned to feel no emotions. So much that teaching self how to hold back the tears was a cake walk. Shit the only time we really acknowledged each other was New Year's but when the morning comes and the day is new things went back to the same shit we knew. A lot of precious moments that was not so precious at all.

Eight honestly I can go on for hours, but to you it may just sound like bitterness. For me its anger because I know the damage that it caused dozens of innocent children. Raised like criminals, treated worse than a slave and to see it still in full effect tells me that. They have brain washed themselves to believe they gave us the best, loved us the hardest, and taught us right.

On the contrary it was the total opposite and it took losing my lifeline their replacement to remember all the many reasons why I never wanted to be a fuck person or parent like that. Worst of all to do it all on purpose.

I love hard because I was taught to hate strong. Now that my age matches the maturity of my mouth I'm shunned away like the devil because I'm a threat for I know too much. See Eight it's always been that way. Divide and conquer for total control. Too bad I was once the house nigga so I knew their souls. I saw the wrong and it's a life of sad stories that goes untold.

Just like the bystanders that stood by and watched me lay on the floor pulling my hair out and knew what caused my pain. There were many on lookers that watched over the years while poor souls were drained leaving shells behind to wander the land with no purpose, destination or plan.

Just like a criminal.

So used to being imprisoned that, that's all you know. So
much so that my heart aches from the pain of knowing all it
takes is a little bit of love and a fighting chance. So it's not
that I let people take advantage of me, for I am the angel no
one sees.......

Wow Storm Eight interjected, not even hearing the
whole story I feel it. I can understand the person you are.
Hiding your good self all the while still giving yourself
selflessly. It takes a special kind of person to carry a heart
so big when all it ever knew was pain.

'Yeah, well I've watched for many years and have taken
note of how the heart felt. The feeling was sickness. How a
family can turn into actors for appearance sake. Well I was
never one to put on an act, especially if it was a living lie

just to make someone look good. Too bad those times were our most enjoyed times.

Over those same years I've watched family ties cut so many times that when you take a closer look they became faded pictures. I think that is what a suicide victims troubles are. They have so much they're holding onto inside, they feel there is no real outlet. Talking doesn't really do it.

That no matter what or how it's said no one will ever really get it. The fact that the only time people say they care is when the person can't hear. So in a way they tell those who know and the rest well in their selfless act they show. So in a way I can relate but the mother in me will never purposely alter my kids' fate...............

Looking back you reflect…

Where there's an ending there's a beginning and a

middle.

Preview of the up coming novel

Quiet!

The crazy part of it all was Master always preached about how his way was in accordance of the law, the law that was in this grand designed book. So I actually went and purchased a copy of this book because I wanted to see for myself, why someone would write such a book. A book that teaches you to actually pick up a real life rod and strike a child. To teach you how to raise a Cane and Able and not a Joab or Ruth.

Well I guess that's why reading let alone education wasn't an important factor. Too bad for them I was born smart and came with more knowledge than they could have ever imagined.

How do you say you love, shower someone with affection then toss them to the side because your idea of deceit is me loving the sisters' and brothers I was giving. You rather we hate each other and harm each other than to care enough to know that your way of dividing us was never right. Or maybe I was just another pawn in the big game of system manipulation.

How else would you reel others in if you didn't have someone to show a lie to. All the while the paper kept rolling in and I got just enough to shut up. Talk about a GRAND DESIGN!!!!!!

To be continued!

Writing this book has been a long journey crawled. Each time it was opened time was spent reading the words over and over so I know in time this will be re-lived by many. I have a good heart naturally and never has there been a time when there has been an ulterior motive. I suffered alone in silence; no one understood my pain or walked through the storm holding an umbrella while I cried. Writing this book was actually more a threat to me than I am harming to the one this will help or hurt. I'm overlooking what a relapse would do because I feel there's always a positive in every negative. My positive is helping someone who finds themselves in the same situation like me not to get where I am four years later. Purposely and unconsciously restricting myself from living life to the fullest because deep down there's a question that even though I know will never be answered haunts me leaving me so stuck feeling hopelessly lost. This is also for the audience which consists of family, friends, associates, etc.....

Anyone who knows someone like me. You hear about many people passing in your lifetime. Yes there is pain, sorrow and grief eventually you come to terms with understanding. But when someone commits suicide there is no understanding and the grief that follows is overwhelming. There is no rule to it and there is no wrong or right way to get over it. Whatever will give you some peace of mind without resorting. Do what you feel will help you. Paying the audience any attention will stunt your healing. I had to choose between keeping family and friends close or keeping my family out of attackers' way. Just remember there will be more time ahead so don't let the little people make this journey harder for you. It's going to be a lot of hurtful things that are going to come out of many people's mouths. No it shouldn't matter but at a time when you need more friends than enemies is really when you see the colors of those that pretend to be close. Everybody knows best and everyone cares less. But no one knew this!

In memory of

James D Jackson III
2-17-73 to 8-1-06